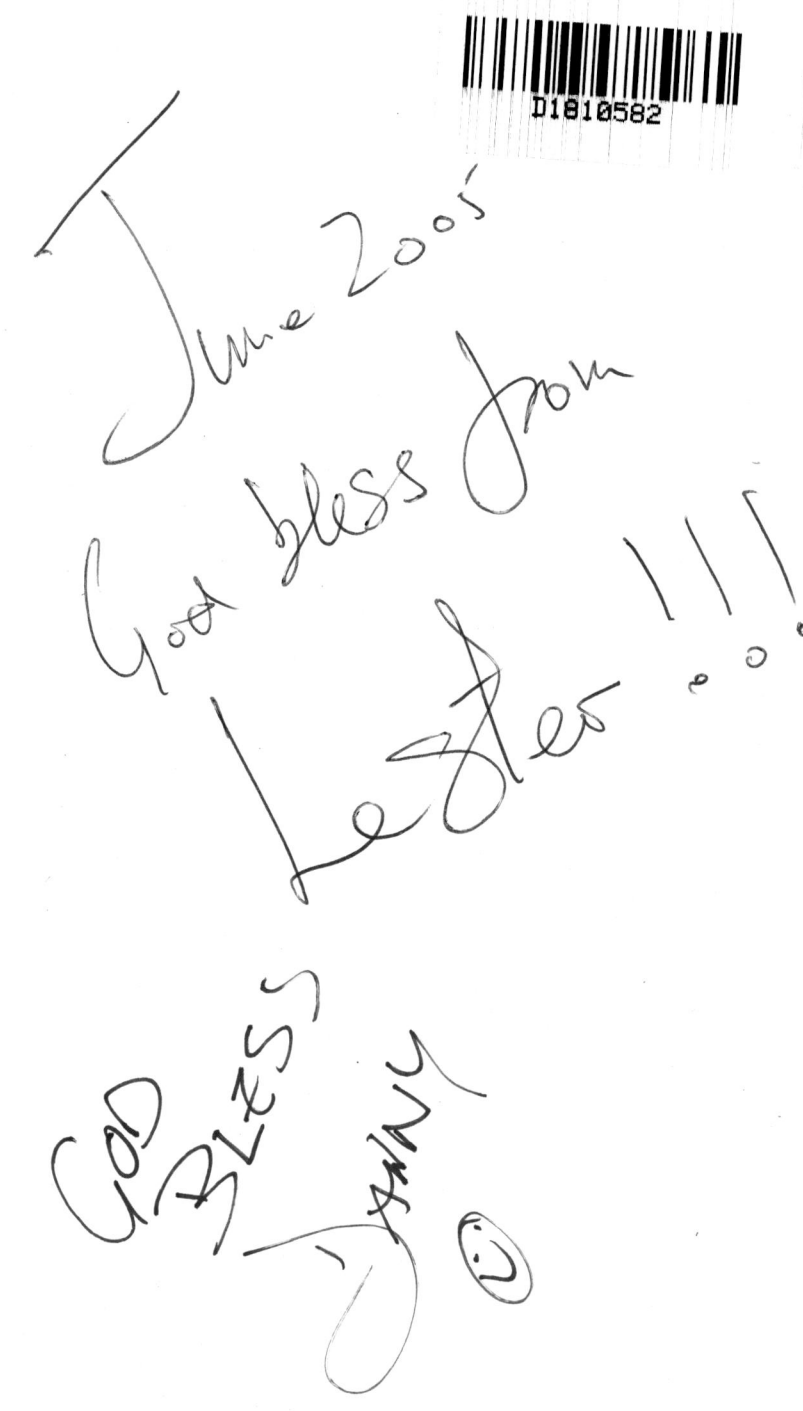

June 2005

God bless from

Lester !!! °°

GOD BLESS JENNY ☺

Aliens Land at Manchester Airport

by

Lester Barr & Daniel Newton

authorHOUSE™

1663 LIBERTY DRIVE, SUITE 200
BLOOMINGTON, INDIANA 47403
(800) 839-8640
WWW.AUTHORHOUSE.COM

© *2005 Lester Barr & Daniel Newton. All Rights Reserved.*

No part of this book may be reproduced, stored in a retrieval system, or transmitted by any means without the written permission of the author.

First published by AuthorHouse 05/02/05

ISBN: 1-4208-2777-4 (e)
ISBN: 1-4208-2776-6 (sc)

Printed in the United States of America
Bloomington, Indiana

This book is printed on acid-free paper.

ONE

Dobber climbed on to the roof of his garden shed. It wasn't difficult because there were two good footholds in the wooden fence beside it.

There was nowhere in the whole wide world that Dobber loved more than the top of that shed. Now before you get the idea that there was something strange about Dobber, let me tell you this. He lived in a place called Moss Nook right beside Manchester Airport, where his father worked as an electrician, looking after the runway lights. And that garden shed was smack bang below the flight path for Runway Two.

Dobber could hear a plane coming in to land. It looked like a Boeing 737. He stood up as tall as he could on that shed roof and stared the Pilot right in the eye as he came in to land. He could feel the heat of the exhaust fumes as it passed overhead. "Oh well" thought Dobber "that's another hole gone in the ozone layer". The fumes left him with a sort of metallic taste in his mouth. In 5 minutes there would be another one. It came into view right on time. "Wicked" thought Dobber. "It's a Turbo-prop". This smaller aircraft came in lower and slower than the big ones and so he could play his favourite game. He stared in through the aircraft windows as it drew level and pulled a strange face at one of the passengers who happened to be looking out at the time. A sort of " - - agghh! I can't breath! help me! I'm choking - -" kind of a face. This always got some reaction.

His real name was Robin Robson. He'd always been a bit embarrassed by his name, and much preferred Dobber: - so even his mum and dad and two sisters called him by his nickname.

Our story begins on an April evening after supper. Dobber had sneaked out of the house to sit on the shed just as it was getting dark. This was the best time to watch planes: after dark. As each jet approached a strong headlight would light up his garden shed, and he would then watch the flashing lights on the wing tips and tail slowly disappear over his garden fence and down on to the runway.

The night was warm, the sky unusually clear. As he stared upwards his thoughts began to wander around the Universe above him. Dreamily he stared at one particularly bright cluster of stars. "I wonder if there's life up there somewhere". He had a feeling that there must be something else beyond his own planet. Somehow he knew that the Universe must contain much more than the familiar things around him on earth. "There must be life somewhere among all those stars and planets above." "Hello.. hello ….

come in planet Zog … can you hear me?" There was no answer.

But what Dobber didn't know was this. Exactly at that moment in time, from that star cluster deep in space, each equally unaware of one another's existence, another Life Form was gazing towards Dobber on planet earth.

TWO

It was a very important meeting. Thousands of life forms had gathered at the edge of a planet in the remote galaxy cluster Abell 22. The planet's name is completely unpronounceable to human beings, and is so far away from earth that it appears only as a small dot on photographs from the Hubble space telescope. The life-forms had come at the request of the High Commander of that sector. There was a sense of excitement among the group, but everything was orderly and calm.

If you had been there to watch them, you would not have seen very much; a little shimmering of light, a little movement of particles of dust at the edge of the planet's atmosphere, and a sense of warmth around you. These particular life forms were quite unlike anything you have seen before.

These life forms are not creatures made of flesh and blood like you and me. They don't need air or water or food for survival, but draw all the energy that they need from cosmic waves and magnetic fields. They don't even live in the same 3 dimensions of space that we live in, which is why they are usually invisible to human eyes.

Instead, they live in a different 3 dimensions. One of their dimensions is time. This means that, for these life forms, moving backwards in time or forwards in time is as easy as stepping to the right or stepping to the left is for you and me. The other 2 dimensions pass inside and outside our own 3 dimensions. This means that they can pass through matter and anti-matter and even through black holes as easily as you or I might splash through shallow water. It also means that they can travel very easily through space and time and then back again. Because they are so different to us it would be better to refer to them as 'life-forces' rather than life forms.

Now that you understand how different these alien life-forces are to us, you will have no difficulty in understanding the command given to them by their High Commander. Their next destination was a small planet many thousands of light years away (earth time) in a solar system in another sector; they were to travel to the edge of the atmosphere of that planet, a planet called "Earth" by those who lived on it. The High Commander pointed towards the solar system to which they would shortly depart.

Among the crowd was one who was particularly impatient to get going. Although still a young life-force at that time, he was full of enthusiasm for the trip ahead. He had already been on a mission with this particular Commander, and so at least had some previous experience of inter-galactic travel. This journey would be difficult. But he looked forward to trying out some of the new powers he could feel growing inside him. He was looking forward to making contact with planet Earth. Hopefully it would contain intelligent life. He gazed longingly into space in the direction of their destination.

THREE

The journey to earth was longer than the young alien life-force had expected, and used up a great deal of his energy. The alien enjoyed the company of the other life-forces travelling with him. They travelled in a strict formation which took a great deal of concentration. They could see the High Commander far ahead, and his guidance for the journey filtered down towards his own group in a sort of rhythmic energy field, a bit like music.

Their arrival at their destination was signalled by a change in the pattern of the music, and the young alien knew he must now wait patiently for further instructions. The High Commander of another sector was already there ahead of them with several thousand life-forces under his command; and more were expected.

Far below him the young alien could see a beautiful blue and green planet, glowing with colour and warmth against the blackness of space. What could be down there?

The young one was not very good at waiting patiently. An appealing thought went through his mind. "Hmmmm. It wouldn't be difficult to slip away unnoticed for a while to get a closer look - just a little closer look at the planet's surface."

Quietly he left the main group and entered earth's atmosphere. The particles of air vibrated around the alien life-force causing a hazy shimmer of light, but his presence, and the presence of the thousands of life-forces above him, could not be detected by any radar system on earth. He got close enough to the planet's surface to pick out all sorts of shades of green and blue and yellow and brown; and then he saw some movement. "Great" he thought, "There's life below." "Maybe I could go closer still to the planet's surface?". Then he remembered "Mmmm. Mind you, I'm not really meant to be this close in the first place!"

"Maybe I shouldn't. After all, someone might notice I was missing. And what if the High Commander returns with further orders? On the other hand, it looks really interesting."

While all of these thoughts were going around, he became aware of a large object coming towards him. It obviously had wings of some sort, with lights flashing at each wing tip, and another light flashing on its tail. Behind the flying creature a trail of wispy cloud appeared looking like a long white streamer painted against the blue sky. The colours of the dawn appeared at the edge of the horizon, as the sun rose in the direction from which the flying object was coming.

It passed within a few metres at great speed, descending towards the planet below. The alien made up his mind immediately. "OK - that's it - here we go! I'm going to follow it down. This looks like FUN!"

The young life-force chased the flying thing through the atmosphere, keeping close behind it. As they both got closer to the ground he became aware of a rise in temperature around him. "This is amazing. The planet is full of life." He stared at the ground below where there was all sorts of movement and activity. "Woops! Keep concentrating! Don't lose the flying creature!" He kept on following it down.

Eventually the flying thing came to a stop on the ground below. The alien watched as some two-legged creatures came out of the craft and walked down some steps. At least two of them carried baskets containing strange hairy 4-legged creatures with long hairy tails. A bright sign was lit up at the top of a building nearby - "WELCOME TO MANCHESTER AIRPORT".

The alien had a good look and a good think. "That big sign over there must be some sort of language. I wonder what it means? And I wonder how that flying thing works? And what about those strange looking creatures? I wonder what the 2-legs and the 4-legs will turn out to be like?"

He was about to find out.

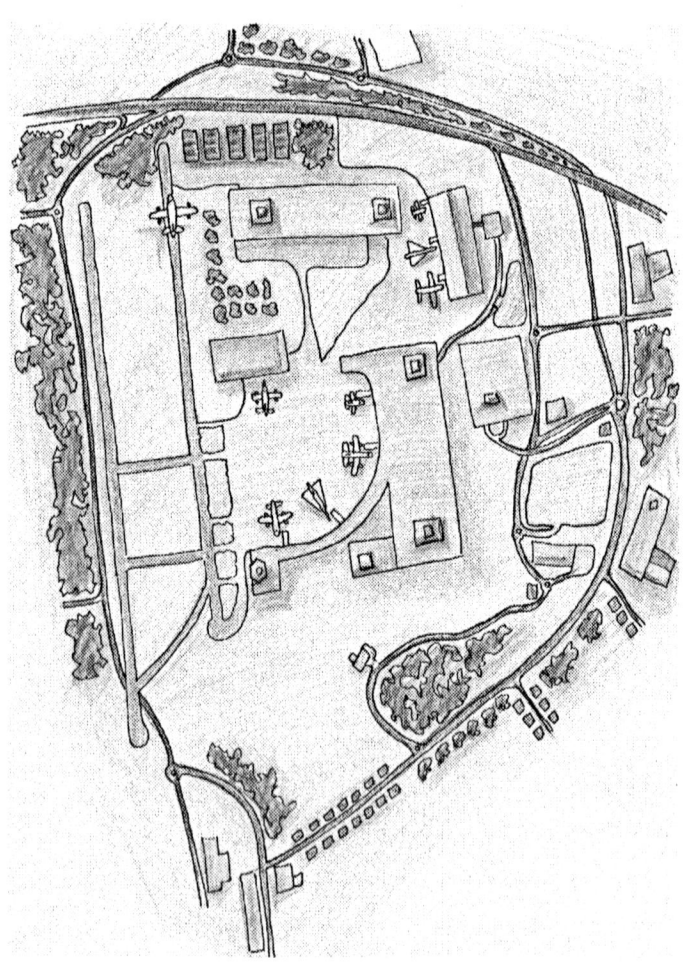

FOUR

One of the favourite tricks of these alien life-forces was to transform themselves into the shape of the most intelligent life form on a particular planet (a process that Dobber would later call 'transmogrifying'). This was the quickest way of obtaining essential data about a new planet. You got to see the best places, hear some great stories, and usually had some adventures along the way. In short, it was much more fun than being invisible.

The alien flew slowly around, taking in all the sights. "Wow. Look at those colours." As the dawn broke the colours in the sky above were totally breath-taking; well they would have been breath-taking to a human like you or me, but of course the alien life-force had no breath to take! He watched several flying objects come and go. "Amazing. The flying things come in all different sizes and designs and colours." He watched them move around on the ground, and every now and again one would pick up speed, take off, and soar into the air.

It was time to transmogrify.

There was a lot of movement going on in one particular building. There was a big banner outside, with letters on it. "I wonder what that one means?" He would have to wait until he knew the language to find out. He went inside. The room was full of 2-legs, and there was lots of activity. This was ideal for the alien.

Now the trick of transmogrifying was to get close to a group of life forms, and then take on a similar molecular structure in such a way as not to be noticed. To do it well, you would choose a group of healthy looking adults, because that way you would transmogrify with an already built in understanding of the language. This saved a lot of work. He was looking forward to learning all about this planet, about the flying craft, about how the language worked, and what the different signs meant.

The young alien would have to wait until some distraction would make everyone look away from his direction. His moment came.

The room was full of noise. There seemed to be hundreds of 2-legs bustling around in there. At the front was a sort of stage, on which were sitting all sorts of shapes and sizes of 4-legs. Suddenly the room went quiet and everyone looked to the front. A group of 2-legs led one of the 4-leg creatures on to a raised platform. A brightly coloured ribbon was placed around its neck, and there was a lot of cheering.

Hopefully no-one would notice the alien transmogrifying while all heads were turned towards the stage. He began the process. Within a few seconds (earth time) he had successfully transformed and taken on a visible form. He was a Cocker Spaniel.

FIVE

The young alien soon realised his terrible mistake. The first clue was the very small vocabulary he found in his transmogrified brain: about 200 variations of woof, whimper and bark. The second clue came when he asked a few questions of a Cavalier King Charles spaniel standing beside him, called Megan. How could he find a 2-leg pet like hers to bring him some food? The mystified look in Megan's face answered his question. The dominant intelligent life forms on this planet were not the 4-legs, but the 2-legged life-forms he had thought were their assistants. The alien asked Megan what the sign outside the door meant. Although she could not read the human's language, she knew of course that it said "DOG SHOW".

This was going to be a problem. He had used up such a large amount of energy in his transformation that it would be several hours or even days before he could repeat the process. This meant that he would have to do things the hard way. He would have to learn the human language from scratch. He would have to communicate with a different species in order to learn how this planet worked - never an easy task.

He would have to find out how the young of the human species learnt their language, and then follow the same learning process.

Luckily Megan knew someone who could help. "Wooaaaarf wuff uwuuff. Wuff woo-owoo wuff" which translated meant "Speak to that dog over there".

It was a Doberman, called Spam. After several minutes of sniffing, whining and barking with him the alien worked out the following. The Doberman lived nearby with a human who had a daughter. Every day this young female human had to go to a place called 'school' and that was where she learnt human language, human tricks, and how to behave as an adult.

The alien knew he would have to find this school.

Spam and Megan took the Cocker Spaniel outside through a side door when no-one was looking. Spam pointed with his nose across the field in front of them to a fence at the edge of the airfield. "The school is 500 dog paces that way" he barked.

The Cocker Spaniel barked a thank-you for this advice and set off toward the school. Spam tried to call him back, explaining that there was no way through the tall fence and that he would have to leave the airport in a car like everyone else. But the transmogrified alien took no notice, wagged his tail, and continued across the field. He soon reached the fence, walked calmly into it and then straight through it, as if it were not there. A little vibration of the wires and a little warmth were the only traces left by the dog on the wire meshing.

SIX

The Cocker Spaniel soon came to a place where lots of young humans were running around at play. The sign above the door read "WELCOME TO PLAY GROUP". It was lunch break and almost everyone was outside. The dog slipped inside unnoticed.

In the first classroom he came to he discovered a large poster on the wall with a list of all the letters he had seen written on signs earlier that day. It began with A and ended with Z, and there were examples of objects beginning with each letter on the poster: a picture, and a word, for each letter of the alphabet. "This is perfect," thought the alien to himself "This must be the code which explains the letters in their alphabet." He quickly memorised this because he knew it must be the basic code of the human language.

He went from classroom to classroom absorbing as much information as he could. Then he slipped out into the playground to hear the children talking. He soon discovered the correct way to pronounce

'DOG' because that's what the children called him. There was a picture of a dog beside the letter D on the alphabet poster. In the same way he learnt how to pronounce A for apple, B for biscuit, C for cup and so on.

Soon he'd worked out the whole alphabet. But this couldn't be the 'school' Spam had told him about. The children were too small. He needed to learn more words. He needed to understand all about the workings of this planet.

The young alien left the Play Group and kept on walking in the direction Spam had indicated. He came to a much larger building with a large blue and purple sign outside it : "MOSS NOOK HIGH SCHOOL". The children here looked much older, and were hanging about in groups around the playground too busy to notice a Cocker Spaniel slip into the school side entrance.

The dog wandered around the classrooms, and found several books. He had a bit of difficulty with the pages, but eventually learned to keep one paw on each side of the opened book and turn the pages with his nose. There were other things that interested him too:- a vending machine for soft drinks; two kids playing badminton in the school gym; a waste paper bin which his doggy nose told him contained 14 different types of smell.

Without warning a bell rang. The alien knew that he had to hide to avoid discovery. Luckily he had spotted a classroom marked BIOLOGY, which had several boxes, and bags piled up against a tank marked 'Handle with care - live frogs'. He stepped carefully over a cage marked "Lizards:- Thomas Atherton" and another marked "Rabbit:- Abigail Turnbull". He kept low, in between a box marked "Cockroaches:- Benjamin Bell" and the frog tank.

The classroom began to fill with excited students and a high volume of noise. Biology lessons didn't always produce this degree of excitement. But today was the first in a series of lessons on 'Sexual reproduction in the animal kingdom'. Mr. Hamill the biology teacher was known to be very entertaining on this subject, and each year his classroom was packed for this particular talk. No-one would be off sick today. It was not unknown for pupils who were not even part of Mr Hamill's class to sneak in at the back. Mr Hamill liked to start this series of lessons with an introductory day in which class members were invited to bring in various creatures, which he would use to explain different points. Last year had been a particular success because a pregnant hamster went into labour during the lesson.

All went well until towards the end of class. A girl called Molly was asked to talk to the rest of the class about her cat, which had given birth to a set of kittens only 2 weeks before.

Molly went over to a cat box marked "Bud the cat". Molly and her family had originally thought that Bud was a male, and had been very surprised when he got pregnant (perhaps they should have come to one of Mr Hamill's lessons). Bud's box was not far

from where the dog was hiding. Molly opened the catch, and pulled out a sleepy black and white cat.

Bud opened her eyes and saw in front of her - a Cocker Spaniel. She flew into a wild frenzy, knocking over her box, then knocking over Molly, hissing furiously at the dog with her hair standing on end.

Now the alien had not yet learned that dogs are meant to chase cats and not the other way round. Fearing for his life he jumped as high into the air as he could. The startled cat and terrified Cocker Spaniel ran around the classroom at high speed under the desks, over the desks, across a work table, scattering homework sheets, pencils and workbooks everywhere. The quick-minded Mr Hamill opened the classroom door and out dashed the dog into the playground as fast as his doggy legs would carry him - closely followed by a string of children trying to catch the Cocker Spaniel, and Molly trying to catch her cat!

The dog found some bushes, darted underneath and kept as quiet as possible. Thankfully the teacher called the chasing children back inside, and the panting spaniel could get his breath back.

Another bell rang, and the children filed out - this time away from the school and not into the playground. The young alien could now relax. Just as he was planning what to do next, a pair of hands reached gently into the bush and pulled him out. It was Dobber.

SEVEN

Dobber had always wanted a dog, and recently had just about got his parents to agree to let him have one. So when he got the spaniel home it didn't take too much persuasion before his parents agreed to let him keep it - at least for a few days until they found its true owner. Dobber's two younger sisters fell in love with the spaniel straight away, and that settled the matter.

Dobber gave the dog half his own dinner, a bowl of water, and three biscuits. He made a sort of basket out of a large cardboard box and some blankets and placed it in his bedroom. Realising this was his home for the night, the transmogrified alien sat down in the box.

Dobber finished his homework, switched off his computer, and packed some books into his bag ready for school tomorrow. He brushed his teeth, brushed the spaniel's ears, and climbed into bed.

The young alien plucked up the courage to try out his English language skills for the first time. "Thanks for looking after me today, Dobber" he said, with a slightly doggy voice.

Dobber's jaw dropped and he nearly fell out of bed with surprise. "A talking dog!" he spluttered. "What the ... how,how,how......y,y,y,y...........y,you can talk!" That was about as much as Dobber could say at that moment. The talking dog took over. "There's no need to look so panicky, Dobber. I need your help. I'd like to be a friend. I've come from the other side of the Universe - so I don't usually look like this! I'm on an important trans-galactic mission, and can only stay a short time."

All feelings of tiredness disappeared, and Dobber and the dog talked together in hushed tones (so as not to wake up his parents) for hours. First the dog talked, explaining his journey from another part of the Universe, explaining that he was usually invisible to human eyes, but could transform into the shape of other life forms.

"Wow. You can transmogrify!" said Dobber - this wasn't a word that the alien could find in Dobber's school dictionary. "Tell me how it's done. Do you have to analyse the life form first, or can you just do it without needing to think or do any calculations?" "Does it hurt?" "And how do you know you're still you when you look like someone else?"

The Cocker Spaniel started a scientific explanation of the process, but then Dobber interrupted .. "Oh, hang on, I'm sorry. I'm asking you all this stuff and have completely forgotten to ask you what your name is. What do people call you?"

"Well, my language is very different to yours. And so my name is totally unpronounceable by humans - let alone a dog! The nearest I can get to explaining my name would be 'impatient-one-who-asks-questions-and-loves-exploring'. That's what my name means"

Dobber wrote this down and began to play with the letters that made up these words. "Hey. Your initials spell IOWAQALE. That sounds quite good. Your name can be Iowa Qale. But I'll call you Qale, for short".

Then Dobber talked. "OK, Qale. You want to know all about our planet. I suggest we go through all the books in my room first, then look up a few things on the Internet using the computer in my room." Dobber picked up a Geography book. He did his best to explain about rainforests, savannahs, tundra and the North and South Poles. Qale had some hard questions. For example, one of the classrooms he'd been in had a project on the wall about a famine in central Africa. "Why do humans in countries with too much food not share more with humans who don't have enough?" "I don't understand that either" agreed Dobber.

Lots of Qale's questions were about the aircraft he had seen. He was fascinated by earth people's technology. "Tell you what, Qale. Let's do a deal. You tell me more about the Universe, and I'll tell you more about Earth. We can start tomorrow by taking a closer look at the aircraft. Tomorrow is Saturday, and I'll take you to the Airport."

But how was he going to smuggle a dog in through the Security checks? Dobber had an idea.

EIGHT

On Saturday morning after breakfast they both went back up to Dobber's room. "OK, Qale" "If we're going to get you through security you'll have to stay hidden and quiet for about 15 minutes while I smuggle you in". Dobber emptied all the heavy books out of a backpack that he used for school. "Try this for size. Jump in". He put the dog inside.

"This is no good" complained a whimpering Qale "I can't see a thing". Dobber had a small knife in his room. "Look, a backpack with a wet nose and pair of eyes staring out of it will look rather suspicious. How about a small peep hole in the side?" Qale agreed and Dobber cut a small hole in his school bag. "Well, fingers and paws crossed. We're off to the Airport."

Dobber knew that a boy with his dog, or just a boy with a rucksack for that matter, would not be allowed anywhere near the main runways or the large passenger aircraft. So Dobber's plan was simple. They would go in to the main terminal buildings with Qale hidden inside the backpack, and then go over to one of the places where his father often worked. "I'm going to take you to a part of the Airport called the 'Aero Flying Club'. It's an amateur club. I know some of the members. The aircraft there are mainly small propeller-driven ones, but at least we can get to see them close at hand."

They slipped through easily into the 'Terminal Two' building. "You can get out of the bag now" said Dobber "no-one's looking. But I'll have to put a collar and lead on you."

"Look at that, Qale. The moving staircase is called an escalator. We'll go up the stairs just beside it". Dobber thought that an escalator would be too confusing for a dog and began to walk up the ordinary stairs.

Just at the last moment Qale jumped onto the up escalator and started climbing. Qale was now travelling twice as fast as Dobber who was on the ordinary stairs - and still attached to his lead. Dobber had to run as fast as he could up the stairs just to keep up.

Qale had enjoyed this ride, and so when they walked passed a moving luggage carousel the spaniel jumped on as quick as a flash. "No..ooo" started Dobber - but it was too late. Dobber found himself dragged along behind the moving Qale. He had to dodge several bits of luggage on the floor. With equally quick thinking, he jumped on the carousel beside the dog. They went round a corner, through a plastic flap, and found themselves outside.

"OK. Don't panic. I know where we are". Qale wasn't panicking. Dobber's heart was racing. Thankfully Dobber knew where they were. "Do you see that grassy runway over there, and a small club hut beside it? That's where we're going. It's the Flying Club." They went over to the hut, and Dobber went inside. There was a small reception window, and Dobber knew the instructor who was behind the desk. "Would you mind if I took a look around the planes? I'd be happy to help with any cleaning or refuelling that needs to be done." "Sure: - go ahead, Dobber. There's at least two of them that could do with a good clean inside. Take a look around, and if you see any jobs that need doing I'll leave it to you to get on with them".

To anyone who passed by over the next couple of hours, he was just a boy and his dog taking a look around and doing some odd jobs. No-one would have believed the truth anyway: an alien disguised as a dog called Qale? And so Qale got to inspect several planes and to sit inside two of them, without ever being disturbed. "Thanks, Dobber. This is great."

Qale had a great trick to help him analyse how things worked. As Dobber looked on in astonishment, Qale passed his paw into the metal of the aircraft as easily as you and I can pass our hands through water. "How did you do that???" Qale stopped for a moment "This is how I can tell what something's made of. I need only a few minutes to analyse the materials." When he took his paw out again there was no hole, no scratch, no mark to show where it had been.

"This is brilliant," said Qale. "The aircraft are made mainly of aluminium, steel and a variety of plastics". "They have a control centre in the cockpit, a communication system, a control system for the wings and rudder, a starting system, a fuel system, sensing devices, safety devices, and back-up systems. The materials are crude but the design and engineering are very clever."

"The most amazing thing" remarked Qale "is that the planes are made 100% of non-flying components. There's nothing in the plane that has the ability to fly all by itself. It's just the clever way in which all the non-flying materials are put together".

The day soon passed. "Do you know Dobber? I'd really like to go flying in one of these." "Aha" said Dobber "That's for tomorrow".

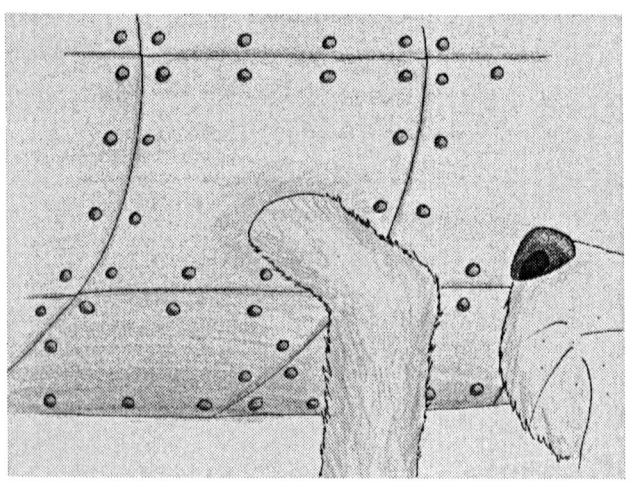

NINE

Sunday morning arrived. At breakfast Dobber asked his father "Dad? Do you think I could telephone Uncle Gavin to see if he would take me flying?" Uncle Gavin was not a real uncle, but had become a family friend over the years as a member of the Aero Flying Club: he had often taken Dobber up for a spin in his plane before.

As it turned out, Uncle Gavin was going flying that very afternoon and would be glad of Dobber's company. Dobber's dad gave the final OK - but explained to Dobber that the spaniel would be better off staying at home.

Dobber prepared a pack lunch (double portions) and waved goodbye - with backpack on his back. Two little eyes looked out from behind the peep hole. Qale wasn't going to be left behind for this adventure; but they couldn't exactly explain to Dobber's dad why not.

Uncle Gavin was already at the club when they arrived, checking that everything was working properly on his twin-engined Piper light aircraft. Dobber climbed aboard and strapped himself in to the seat behind Gavin, placing the backpack on the seat next to him in such a way that Qale could get a good view of everything. Soon the engines revved up, and Uncle Gavin had them climbing upwards into the clouds. The views were amazing and the flight was fantastic.

For 20 minutes or so everything went perfectly, until without warning they hit an air pocket. The aircraft dropped suddenly by several meters, the backpack flew up off the chair, the catch came undone, and Qale dropped out of the bag head first into the co-pilots chair.

Gavin didn't seem particularly alarmed at this, and told Dobber that he had a very cute dog. "Thanks Uncle Gavin" Dobber replied "This really is a brilliant flight".

Without thinking, the Cocker Spaniel in the co-pilot's chair added "Yeah, thanks. This really is brilliant".

Uncle Gavin went quite pale at first, then a sort of yellowy green, and then closed his eyes and slipped off his chair on to the floor - unconscious from the shock of what he'd just heard. The plane began to take a nosedive downward, and then to spin rather alarmingly. "Wake up Gavin!" "Wake up ….. wake up ….. wake up!!" It was useless. He was in a complete faint.

There was only one thing to do. Qale grabbed the steering wheel, and making some adjustment to the controls with his nose managed to make the plane level off again and resume flying smoothly. "Don't panic, Dobber. I've been watching Gavin at the controls, and know the airplane well enough to fly this thing now myself. You might have to help me with some of the switches. They're not exactly designed for twiddling by paw."

"I think we'd better get down straight away" said Dobber "in case he needs a doctor". "OK" said Qale "I'll turn the plane back towards the runway and head for the Flying Club."

They flew in low across the airport, passing just in front of the main control tower. The air-traffic-controller on duty was looking out of his observation window just as a twin-engined 4-seater Piper light aircraft flew by. He could see the pilot clearly - a Cocker Spaniel. Behind the pilot - the face of a boy peering out of the passenger window. He took off his glasses, wiped them twice, and rang his boss - he didn't feel very well, and would have to go home at once.

TEN

The following day was Monday. "Great" said Qale "Can I come to school with you?" "OK. But if I'm going to smuggle you into school you'll have to promise to be quiet and not get me into trouble." "I'll put you in my backpack again, and try and position you so that you can see the front of the classroom through the spy hole. But remember - no talking - and don't answer any questions if the teacher at the front asks us something!"

The day went well. Maths, English, Geography, History, - Qale loved them all. Everything went smoothly. Until Biology. It was Benjy's turn for audience participation. He had a cockroach in a matchbox, and he enjoyed the groans and muffled screams from his classmates (mainly the girls) as he took it out. To make things more interesting, Benjy gave it a flick with his finger to make it fly. Off it went.

A buzzing flying cockroach went twice round the room. Everyone ducked then got under their desks.

The cockroach looked for somewhere safe to hide and chose - Dobber's backpack. In it flew buzzing angrily. Out flew Qale. Cocker Spaniel, cockroach, children, teacher - all went into a spin around the classroom; someone opened the door; and everyone spilled out of the classroom.

Everyone that is except the cockroach. Mr Hamill had managed to swat it with a biology book, and dispose of it in the bin. Dobber felt sorry for the squashed cockroach, and when no-one was looking rescued it out of the bin, and put it back into its matchbox.

That night in Dobber's room, Dobber and Qale took the cockroach out of the box to have a good look at it.

"What should I do with this cockroach, Qale? Do you think I should bury it? Maybe I should give it back to Benjy for some sort of funeral? Mind you, knowing his sense of humour, it would probably end up in someone's lunch box. So perhaps that's not such a good idea. Why don't you have a look at it?"

Qale passed his paws over it so that he could find out how it worked, and did an analysis of its wings just like he'd done with the plane. "This is incredible," said Qale. "It's only a fraction the size of Gavin's plane, but it too has a control centre, a communication system, a fuel system, sensing devices, and back-up systems. You humans are really amazing to have built something like this".

Dobber thought this was very funny! "NO, NO. You've got it completely wrong. Humans don't make cockroaches!!".

Qale continued his analysis. "You're right" he said "It's much more complex than the plane. It's made of millions of tiny cells, and nothing like the crude metals of the plane. So who has made these?".

Dobber tried to explain. "Well, no-one has made them. The cockroach has come about by evolution - the forces of nature working on different chemicals over millions of years." Qale scratched his head. "This is really a strange planet. In every other planet I have ever visited the random forces of nature tend to make things come apart, not join together in such brilliantly clever design. Perhaps the laws of the Universe are different on Earth?" Qale thought some more - "Tomorrow, I'm going to do some exploring of my own."

ELEVEN

On Tuesday Dobber went to school on his own, and got home around 4 o'clock. He was greeted by an excited dog. "Welcome back, Dobber. How was school?""Pretty boring, really. Much less exciting than yesterday's cockroach chase. I've been day-dreaming all day, wondering what you've been up to."

Qale took him at once into the garden.

There in a long row stood various objects all lined up neatly behind his dad's car. "What on earth have you done here, Qale?" There was a doggy smile from Qale.

"Tell me what you see, Dobber"

"Well, starting from the shed —- there's a couple of old wheels …. then there's a wheelbarrow …… then my old scooter …. then a kids bike …… then Mum's bicycle ….. then a tricycle …… then a skateboard …..then a few toy cars …..then Dad's car ….. and sitting on the bonnet, you've got a model aircraft."

"Aha! said Qale "it's WHEEL EVOLUTION!".

"**One** wheel on a wheelbarrow, **two** wheels on a scooter, **three** on a tricycle, **four** on a car and **five** on this plane. You humans invented the wheel, and then all these things have evolved from it."

"So tell me, Dobber – how did the plane come into being? Did a car just grow wings??"

Dobber looked puzzled. "No, of course not. Someone thought of the idea and then built it."

"Well" said Qale. "If someone has carefully designed and engineered the aircraft, who has made the cockroach? It's massively better designed!"

"Evolution made it" said Dobber "You know. Trial and error. Survival of the fittest and all that."

"That doesn't make sense!" Qale passed his paw through the metal door of Dad's car and opened the locks. "Come inside the car!" He jumped on to the passenger seat. Dobber opened the driver's door and sat behind the steering wheel.

"I can see that you need Evolution on your planet to help animals adapt to changes in the environment – a bit like wheel evolution. But that doesn't explain how all the complex design got into each animal - or into this car - in the first place!"

These words took Qale 19 seconds to say. Dad's car alarm was timed to go off 20 seconds after an intrusion.

Beeeeeeeeeeeeeeeeeeeeeepeeeeeeeeeeeeeeee eeeeepeeeeeeeeeeeeeeeeeeepeeeeeeeeeeeeeeee eeeeeeepeeeeeeeeeeeeeeeepeeeeeeeeeeeeeeep

Qale jumped out of the car and on to the skateboard. With three paws to balance himself, his fourth paw went furiously back and forth to help his escape – out of the garden gate.

The lady next door looked out of her window to where the noise was coming from. She saw a dog speeding down the road on top of a skateboard; stopping at the traffic lights; and then speeding off again when the lights turned green. She turned pale; then phoned the police. The police officer asked if the skateboard had a registration plate. It didn't. She put the phone down and went to bed.

TWELVE

The following day was Wednesday. Qale went for a long walk and then came home to do more tests on the cockroach.

When Dobber got home from school, Qale was watching TV. "How are you getting on?" asked Dobber. "Well, no matter how hard I try I just can't get the hang of these cartoons. You need to have a Dobberish sense of humour for those. Star Trek is OK, but not like the real thing. My favourite is definitely the weather forecasts ….. they always make me laugh!"

"I actually meant, how are you getting on with the cockroach?"

Qale took him upstairs. Carefully they opened the matchbox, and looked inside.

"I've made an important discovery about the cockroach". "Just like the plane, it's made up 100% of non-flying components. There's some brilliant engineering in here which puts the components all together in such a way so as to make it live and

53

make it fly. Inside each cell is a code containing the instructions which makes it all work. The code is a language, just like the letters of your alphabet. The language isn't English. But it is a language that I recognise, Dobber".

Dobber wanted to know more. "You recognise it? So what's it like?"

"Your English alphabet has 26 letters, arranged into words which have meanings. The words are lined up in sentences. The alphabet that I've found in the cockroach has 4 letters - arranged into words and sentences, and then twisted into a spiral shape to make them fit into the cell. The words are instructions, telling the cells how to make cockroach components and how to fit them all together and make them work."

Dobber knew what he was talking about, as he had seen a website about 'genes' on his computer. He switched on his PC, and soon a spiral-shaped picture of a 'gene' appeared on the screen. He was able to fill in some of the technical jargon for Qale. "The letters of the alphabet are known as DNA. The words and sentences?- - They're called genes."

"Thanks, Dobber. It looks like my analysis has picked up the DNA language. It's a very beautiful language which produces a sort of spiral-shaped music when you speak it. Listen. I'll give you an example."

Qale cleared his throat, and several dollops of dog spit sprayed across the room towards Dobber, and Dobber's PC. He lifted his head towards the ceiling.

"Owooooooo-wuuurfawoooooaaaaaghuu-uu-aoo – aooo awoooo plehuhuhuhuh ahoo ahuwoo ooooooooooooooooooooooooooooooo"

A dreadful piercing howling noise filled the house. Dobber dived for cover under his bed, with both hands over his ears. He slid across a blob of dog spit on the carpet.

They heard footsteps running up the stairs. It was Dobber's Mum. She burst in through the door "What's going on Dobber? What's that noise? What on earth are you up to?" His sisters' faces peered in through the door behind them. Dobber had to think quickly.

"Nothing Mum. It's just the computer. The dog's dribbled on the keyboard". Dobber picked up the keyboard and some doggy slime ran off the edge. Dobber's Mum didn't look completely convinced, but the noise had stopped, and everything looked OK. She and the children went downstairs.

"That was close" said Qale. "I'm afraid that dog vocal cords aren't designed for singing." Qale paused for a moment, and had a look on his face of the kind you get when you're doing mental arithmetic. Not that dogs often do mental arithmetic.

"Dobber. I need to do one more experiment. Pass me some of your hairs."

"What?? No way. You must be joking."

"Oh go on! Just a little bit of hair!" Before Dobber had a chance to object again, Qale jumped up and took a mouthful of hair from just above his left ear.

"Ouch!!"

"Thanks, Dobber. I only need a few". Qale passed his paw through the collection of hairs. "Now pass me my dog brush, please." Dobber helped Qale remove a few dog hairs from the brush, and once again Qale ran his paw through them.

"I'll tell you something interesting, Dobber. Humans, dogs, cockroaches: all are made up of tiny cells. And the instructions inside them are written in the same DNA language no matter what species you are".

"Now I'll tell you something weird. It's a language that I recognise. A spiral, containing 4 letters arranged in pairs. It's my own language, Dobber, my own language from the other side of space. It's the language that I speak with my friends."

Qale had found the words of his own language written down inside each cell that he analysed. "The language used in these cells is the language spoken by me, by all my fellow life-forces, by my High Commander, and by the Commander of all High Commanders."

Dobber at first couldn't understand how a language spoken at the other side of the Universe could have become written down within the DNA of the life forms on such a small and distant planet.

"There's only one way in which my language could have come to be inside each cell of each living thing on your planet."

"What is it?"

Dobber sensed that they had stumbled across a deep truth. Some common force must bind together Dobber and Qale across the Universe. There must be some common Truth, some common Intelligence, that had brought both of them into being and had now brought them together as friends.

"This language must have been given to you by the The Commander of All High Commanders. He must have given you life in the same way that He has given us life."

Qale had discovered that Earth was no different from other planets. Every living thing, including the cockroach, contained the Words spoken by the Infinite Father of All Things, the Commander of All High Commanders, when He created them.

THIRTEEN

It was now around midnight.

"Dobber, the time has come for me to go. I must join the rest of my group again." Quietly, Dobber nodded his head. "Say 'thank you' to your mum, dad and sisters. They've been very kind to me over the last few days." Together they went outside into the garden, and clambered on to the roof of the garden shed. Dobber knew that this would be the last time he saw his friend.

They talked for a while. "Why have you come here, Qale?" Qale looked thoughtful - "I don't know why so many of us have been summoned here, Dobber. But I've sensed that some dark forces are at work on your planet. It's such a beautiful place - and yet there is so much hatred and cruelty in your world … war, violence, pollution, selfishness. You humans seem to have lost touch with the Infinite Father who made you."

Dobber agreed. "I wonder if He's so fed up with the mess we've made of His beautiful planet, that

He is about to wrap it all up before we destroy it completely?"

"Could be. I sense a battle is already underway for your planet."

As he spoke these words, the Cocker Spaniel changed in appearance before his eyes, from being dog-shaped, to something much taller and stronger and human-like, but extremely bright and somehow transparent. He seemed to float upwards away from the shed, and then picked up speed accelerating powerfully upwards into the dusk sky. Dobber could see his bright form for several minutes, and then he seemed to be joined by thousands of other similar life-forces in the sky. Above the noise of an aircraft taking off from Manchester Airport he could just make out the sound of music.

The months passed, and Dobber never saw Qale again. But on Christmas Eve something strange happened which he would never forget.

There was an envelope waiting for him on the doorstep – with a paw print on it. Inside he found a Christmas card. It was a picture of angels in a night sky over the village of Bethlehem. And although it was only a drawing, Dobber recognised the expression on the smallest angel's face at once. It was Qale.

END

FOURTEEN
The Science Behind The Story

What are genes?

A gene is a bit like a computer programme. Think of your computer at school or at home. It may have a word-processing programme, a dictionary, a spell-checking programme, a calculator, an e-mail programme, an internet browsing programme, all linked together to make your computer work. The programmes that make our bodies work are called genes. We have about 35,000 in total. Perhaps you have a gene that has given you blue eyes, or short legs, or straight hair, and so on:- your genes contain the instructions that make all the different parts of your body. They tell the billions of cells (of which we are made) how to fit together and how to work together.

Where are our genes?

Take a look at your hands. Skin, nails, muscles, tendons, bones, blood vessels, movement, sensation.

Now look closer using a magnifying glass. Fingerprint ridges in the skin, sweat pores, hair follicles. Now look closer still using a microscope. Every one of these structures is made of tiny cells. And inside these cells you will find a blob in the middle called the nucleus. Inside the nucleus you will find your genes.

What is DNA?

Our genes are made out of stuff called DNA. It's a complex chemical, which has a spiral shape when you look at it under a powerful microscope.

What is the genetic code?

Your computer programmes use a 2-digit 'digital' code, made from electronic signals. Genes use a 4-digit code, made from the 4 different chemical components of DNA. These 4 chemicals are like the letters of an alphabet. A typical gene might contain 5000 separate letters, which are strung together in a great big long line just like the words on this page. A gene is thus like a chapter in an instruction manual; several chapters are then joined together to form a chromosome. A chromosome contains as much information as a typical encyclopaedia, and you have 46 chromosomes in every nucleus in every one of your cells (23 pairs).

What is a DNA fingerprint?

Each gene has its own function, and all human beings are made from the same genetic instructions. Thankfully there are also lots of variations within those basic instructions, which is why we are all a bit different. These variations can be analysed in a technique known as DNA fingerprinting, which can be very useful in identifying a criminal suspect. The identity of a suspect can be worked out just from a few hairs discovered at the scene of the crime.

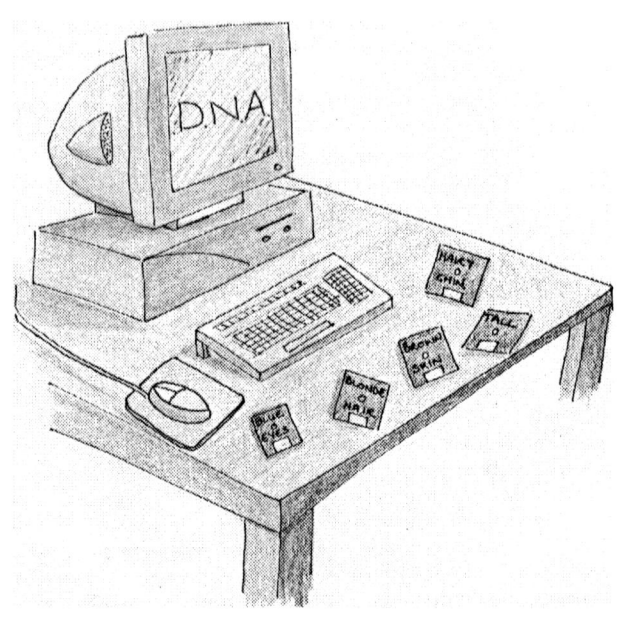

What is a mutation?

If the sequence of letters of the DNA code is altered, this is called a mutation. It is like a spelling mistake in a book or computer programme.

Where did all the information written in our genes come from?

The most popular explanation at present is that it came there as a result of evolution. The basic theory is easy to understand:- survival of the fittest. This can cause changes in the size or colour or features of an animal in response to changes in the environment. A harder thing for evolution to explain is how simple things become more complex, and how new design features emerge such as legs or wings or lungs. The theory is that gene mutations can cause this; perhaps some mutations may be good and others bad, and the 'survival of the fittest' principle will make the good ones flourish.

But modern gene research has produced some surprises.

1. The genes, which drive our cells, are amazingly complex; even more complex than the programmes driving our computers. The way in which our computers have evolved since they were first invented has not happened by chance – but by careful thought. Our computers are clearly the product of intelligence, of careful design, of clever

manufacturing techniques. The level of design within our genes strongly suggests that they too have been designed by an Intelligence.

2. Thousands of mutations have been found in crucial human genes, but none of them make things work better. They are either neutral or cause gene malfunction. If evolution was indeed driven by gene mutation, you would expect to see many complex innovative mutations emerging. You don't. Random mutations tend to make things worse, not better. This makes sense. If you put mutations into the instructions in your computer, it makes things malfunction - it never produces clever new programmes.

3. Think about domestic animals. Maybe you have a pet dog. All dogs have come from a common wolf-like ancestor. Human selection has made them evolve into all sorts of different shapes and sizes and breeds; but they are still all dogs; with 4 legs, a tail, and a wet nose. Intense selection has not produced new design features. Quite the opposite. The more you select, the weaker that breed becomes. The gene pool picks up more harmful disease; it does not become stronger and fitter.

Facts such as these run in the opposite direction to the atheism that lies behind a lot of evolutionary teaching.

For hundreds of years Jews, Christians and Moslems have been consistently saying the same thing; the stuff of which we are made has been designed and created. Our DNA has been designed. The evolutionary mechanisms within DNA have been designed. The science of genetics is not on the side of the atheist.

The hidden message in the secret code.

DNA is a code, a complex language, a vast collection of cleverly combined computer programmes. It contains this hidden message: – Like all codes, like all languages, like all computers, it too has been designed. It too has been created. It is not the product of random mutation. It is the work of an Intelligence beyond all intelligence.

ABOUT THE AUTHOR

Lester Barr and Daniel Newton both live near Manchester Airport in England. Lester is a cancer specialist; his hobby is genetics. Daniel is the illustrator; his hobbies are cricket, football and playing drums.

Printed in the United Kingdom
by Lightning Source UK Ltd.
104832UKS00001B/214-303